CHRISTMAS
IN
NEW YORK CITY

TEXT
Francis Morrone

ILLUSTRATIONS
Shauna Mooney Kawasaki

GIBBS·SMITH
P
PUBLISHER

SALT LAKE CITY

ISBN 0-87905-615-0
This is a Peregrine Smith book,
published by
Gibbs Smith, Publisher
P. O. Box 667
Layton, Utah 84041

95 94 93   10 9 8 7 6 5 4 3 2 1

Copyright © 1994
Gibbs Smith, Publisher

All rights reserved.

Printed and bound in Hong Kong

'Twas the night
before Christmas
and all through
Manhattan,

Queens, Brooklyn,
and Bronx,
and the Island
called Staten.

There creeped
over brownstones
a guy dressed
as Claus—

a fake!
an imposter!
a jerk
who broke laws!

At that
very moment
from Upstate
there flew

true Santa,
sleigh, toys,
and his pro
reindeer crew.

Soaring over
the Hudson
through
billowing snow,

he swooped
over Macy's,
his cheeks
all aglow.

Then Santa
climbed down a
Park Slope
chimney stack.

"Hands up!"
police bellowed,
"You Santa Claus
quack."

With the clink
of the steel,
the Jolly One
shivered.

Could it be
that the presents
might not
get delivered?

But wait!
Two young children
had viewed
the commotion.

Saving Santa
from Sing-Sing
would take
a great notion.

They knew
the police chief
had nabbed
the wrong guy,

but who
could give Santa
a strong
alibi?

They donned
their warm coats,
ventured into
the street.

They'd collar
that thief
through the snow,
through the sleet!

Through the
pigeons and ice,
they wandered
about

underneath
Brooklyn Bridge
where a voice
cackled out:

"You shouldn't
be here!"
said the man
wrapped in rags,

with all
his belongings
in two
shopping bags.

"But Santa's
in prison!
They think
he's the crook!

"We must
find the thief
and the stuff
that he took."

"'Tis so?"
croaked the stranger,
"'Tis sad,
and 'tis tragic.

" I'm Clement Clark
Moore, though.
I'll help with
Yule magic.

"I am
no longer living—
I am
spook, specter, ghoul.

But I'm lured back
for Christmas
by Gotham's
rare Yule.

"On, Lassie!
On, Laddie!
We must seize
this louse

and the presents
he took
from co-op
and house.

"Let us fly!
To the subway!
Express IRT!"

They went
roaring uptown
as swift as
could be.

To the
Empire State
lit with
red and green glows,

up to
floor 102
of The Building
they rose.

Clem ushered
the kids
to his
favorite scope.

He slipped
in a quarter
and gave them
all hope.

They peered
through the lens
over rooftop
and street

and found
what they sought
through the snow
and the sleet.

Down there!
Rockefeller's
grand tree
trimmed in ice;

some smooth,
gliding skaters;
then scenes
not so nice:

on Broadway,
in costume,
right out
on display,

was a guy
dressed as Claus
who was not
in a play.

They rushed
to Fifth Avenue
in cold
Christmas air,

and Clem
flagged a cabbie:
"Quick! on to
Times Square!"

In the glitz
and the neon,
the kids and
old Clem

pounced upon
thieving Santa,
and out fell
a gem.

The cops
swarmed around them
and heard
the whole tale,

then radioed in:
"Let St. Nick
out of jail!"

Soon Santa
could say
as his reindeer
took flight:

"Merry Christmas,
Big Apple.
It's been
quite a night!"